THE CRUNCHBONE CASTLE CHRONICLES

QUEEN CARRION'S BIG BEAR HUG

Karen Wallace

illustrated by Helen Flook

A & C Black • London

For Stirling Spowers

First published 2006 by
A & C Black Publishers Ltd
38 Soho Square, London, W1D 3HB

www.acblack.com

Text copyright © 2006 Karen Wallace
Illustrations copyright © 2006 Helen Flook

The rights of Karen Wallace and Helen Flook to be identified as the
author and illustrator of this work have been asserted by them in
accordance with the Copyrights, Designs and Patents Act 1988.

ISBN 0-7136-7556-X
ISBN 978-0-7136-7556-6

A CIP catalogue for this book is available from the British Library.

This book is produced using paper that is made from wood grown in
managed, sustainable forests. It is natural, renewable and recyclable.
The logging and manufacturing processes conform to the
environmental regulations of the country of origin.

Printed and bound in Great Britain by Bookmarque Ltd, Croydon

Chapter One

King Cudgel howled at the top of his voice and scrambled onto a rock. The bear scrambled after him, roaring louder.

Then it stretched out a huge paw and caught King Cudgel's purple velvet pantaloons with its claws.

The king howled again but this time it was with a mixture of terror and despair. They were his favourite pantaloons and had turquoise bunnies embroidered down the seams. It would be too terrible if they were ripped!

Suddenly, the bear dragged him down and flung its great, hairy arms around his neck. King Cudgel waited for the moment when he would feel the first, sharp points of its huge teeth sink in.

But it didn't happen like that. Instead he felt the bear's hot, berry-flavoured breath on his face.

'Help me!' it pleaded. 'Help me!'

∞

Quail, the king's trusty servant, put down the tea tray. On the other side of the room, King Cudgel was rolling about under his bedclothes and shouting, 'How? How?' at the top of his voice.

'Your Majesty,' said Quail, taking a firm hold of the bedclothes and pulling hard. 'Wake up! It's only a dream!'

A second later, King Cudgel tumbled onto the floor and landed on a thick, fleecy rug. He lay there for a moment, his eyes rolled back in his head, and then, with shaking legs, he heaved himself up and fell back onto the bed.

'Oh dear, oh dear,' said Quail in his most soothing voice. 'Another of your bad dreams, sire? Which one was it this time?'

'It was the bear dream,' whispered King Cudgel. 'Thing is, Quail, I've been having it every night for two weeks!'

As he spoke, the king sat up and held out his arms like a scarecrow as Quail helped him into a yellow, spotted shirt and a pair of yellow, spotted pantaloons.

'I'm sure it means something,' said the king, as he squeezed his thin, pointed feet into a pair of blue suede ankle boots. 'I'm *positive* it does.'

'Of course it means something, sire,' said Quail, trying not to sound impatient. 'It means you've been eating too many sugar lumps before you go to sleep.'

As Quail walked over to the king's jacket wardrobe, he caught sight of a picture of Queen Carrion hanging on the wall. Two fierce, brown eyes stared out of a heavy, snarling face.

Quail let his mind go back to the time of the queen's mysterious disappearance almost a year ago and thought, as he often did, that in some ways things were much quieter at Crunchbone Castle since she'd been gone.

The queen's bad temper was legendary and the swear words that streamed out of her mouth had often turned the air purple. Even so, ever since the fateful morning she mistook her sword for a walking stick and went out bear hunting on her own, her presence in the castle had been missed.

Of course the royal children, Prince Marvin and Princess Gusty Ox, were pretty good at looking after themselves. It was King Cudgel who needed the attention. He was famous throughout the land for being a flashy dresser and changed his outfit at least four times a day.

And that meant a lot of work for one particular person.

Quail.

The king's trusty servant eased a yellow, spotted jacket from its hanger. 'Your Majesty,' he began. Then he stopped.

King Cudgel was staring at the portrait of his wife, his cheek muscles twitching in his white face. In fact, his whole body was shaking so much that his blue suede ankle boots made a noise on the stone floor as if he was tap dancing.

'Your Majesty!' said Quail, again. He dropped the jacket. 'What on earth is wrong?'

'The queen,' mumbled King Cudgel, unable to take his eyes off the portrait. 'The bear in my dreams is the queen!' He held his head in his hands. 'The eyes are the same! The snarl is the same! Even her breath smelled the same!' King Cudgel looked up. 'But what does it mean, Quail? What does it *mean*?'

Quail had never seen his master in such a state. This was definitely a matter for the court wizard. 'Summon Crackle!' he said firmly. 'He'll know what to do!'

'Quail!' cried the king. 'You're a genius!' He jumped up and was about to ring the large, silver hand bell he kept on his dressing table when he stopped, his hand in midair. 'There's only one problem.'

'What?' asked Quail, suspiciously. He couldn't think of any problem.

The king waved a fretful hand at his outfit. 'The yellow, spotted look,' he said anxiously. 'I don't think it's quite right for such a serious moment, do you?'

Quail dropped the jacket on the floor and tried not to scream.

Chapter Two

Crackle, disguised as a frog, was sunning himself on a lily pad, when Quail suddenly appeared. 'Get up, you lazy toad!' he shouted, taking out all his frustration with the king on the wizard. 'Don't you ever work for a living?'

Crackle opened one skinny, green eye. 'Of course I do,' he croaked, lazily. 'Very hard, as it happens. And for your information, I'm a frog not a toad.'

'You're a lazy lump as far as I'm concerned,' yelled Quail, who had just spent the last hour re-dressing the king from top to bottom and from inside out in black velvet with red stripes. 'Get up! The king wants to see you! It's an emergency!'

Crackle wiggled a froggy leg in the soupy, brown water. 'It's always an emergency,' he sighed. 'What is it this time?'

'Queen Carrion!' cried Quail. 'He's seen her in a dream!'

'*What*?' shouted Crackle. He leapt from the lily pad as a frog and landed as a wizard on the grass. 'Why didn't you say so?'

'Because you didn't ask,' snapped Quail. 'And you'd better hurry, I've never seen him in such a state!'

'I tell you, Crackle,' said King Cudgel after he had repeated his dream for the fifth time. 'It's her! I know it is! And she needs my help.' He frowned. It was the first time in his life he had ever felt like this about his wife. 'What should I do?' he asked hopelessly.

The king wasn't the only one who was feeling hopeless. In fact, Crackle was feeling terrified. He was sure Queen Carrion was the bear in the king's dreams, but after that he didn't know what to do about it.

'Summon Prince Marvin and Princess Gusty Ox!' said Crackle quickly. 'We must consult the steam from the magic kettle.'

King Cudgel pouted. 'But last time you did that I couldn't see anything.'

'Of course you couldn't,' replied Crackle sharply. 'You're a king not a wizard.'

'All right, all right,' said the king wearily. 'I don't care what you do as long as you do something fast.'

Five minutes later, Prince Marvin and his twin sister, Princess Gusty Ox, ran into the room. The royal children had been about to sit down to breakfast in Prince Marvin's snack shack – the prince had given up horse riding and taken up cooking instead – when Quail told them the news.

Now they stood, their stomachs rumbling with hunger yet fizzing with excitement, as Crackle lit a small camping stove and put what looked like an old, rusty kettle on top of it.

A silence fell in the room as everyone watched the steam from the kettle form a square, rather like a television set, and hang wobbling in the air.

'Wow!' said Princess Gusty Ox as Crackle stepped forward and peered into the square. 'What can you see?'

To Crackle's horror, he saw nothing except a load of jagged lines. 'Nothing,' he mumbled. 'Bad reception.'

'So what are you going to do?' demanded the king.

'I'll try the magic biscuit tin,' said Crackle, pulling out a large, metal box from the folds of his cloak. 'It always works.' He looked nervously at King Cudgel. 'A picture appears on the back of the lid, you see.'

But even though Crackle stood over the biscuit tin and waved his wand and said his most complicated spells, which sounded to Quail like *abracadabra*! backwards, nothing happened.

Crackle gulped and felt his stomach fill with ice cubes. The moment he had dreaded all his life had finally arrived. Queen Carrion must have fallen under a really powerful spell if neither the kettle nor the biscuit tin came up with an answer. Crackle knew his only chance was to use his most complicated spell. And that meant he would have to burn his favourite, pointy hat and wait for the answer to appear in the smoke.

Without a word of explanation, Crackle took off his hat, put it down on the stone floor and set fire to it.

'Behold the pictures in the smoke,' he cried and stepped to one side.

The king and the royal children stared in amazement. First they saw themselves in a family group. It was unbelievable! Queen Carrion was in the middle and everyone was smiling!

Then another picture appeared. The king, Quail and the prince and princess were standing in a dark forest. In front of them a bear that looked like Queen Carrion was standing beside Queen Carrion who looked like a bear!

They were identical!

At that moment, the flames from Crackle's favourite, pointy hat died away. A silver arrow lay in the ashes.

Nobody spoke and Crackle felt his mind spin! Suddenly he understood what everything meant.

The wizard stood in the middle of the great hall. 'Listen to me!' he cried. 'And I will tell you what has happened to the great Queen Carrion!'

The room went so quiet you could have heard a flea sniff, as Crackle explained how the forest was ruled by a wicked witch in the shape of a bear and how she had put a spell on the queen.

'The Bear Witch always wanted to be a queen,' cried Crackle. 'So on that fateful day when Queen Carrion only had a walking stick to defend herself, the Bear Witch tried to turn her into a bear. But the great queen was so strong she fought back and so the Bear Witch's spell only half worked.'

'Is that why our mother only half looks like a bear?' asked Prince Marvin.

Crackle nodded.

'What can we do to save her?' asked King Cudgel. He swallowed. 'She needs our help. I know she does.'

'The Bear Witch must be stabbed with the silver arrow,' said Crackle. 'Then

Queen Carrion will become herself again, the Bear Witch will disappear and her power over the forest will be over.'

'But my mother and the Bear Witch both look the same!' cried Princess Gusty Ox. Since she was the only one in her family who could aim or even throw straight, it was pretty obvious that the job of using the arrow would be hers. 'How will we tell the difference?'

'You will know when the time comes,' replied Crackle, mysteriously. He strode across the room and pointed to the sky. 'What's more, you see that the moon is almost full.' He turned and let his sparkling eyes sweep across the room. 'It is almost a year to the day since the queen disappeared. She must be freed from the spell before the moon becomes full again and a second year begins. Otherwise she is doomed to remain half bear, half human for ever!'

Chapter Three

King Cudgel stood nervously in the castle yard, beside a cart overloaded with trunks and boxes and his own private tent. It had been a long time since he had been on any kind of expedition and he was not good at travelling light.

'Did you pack my woolly pyjamas and my quilted, silk dressing gown with the leopard-skin collar?' he asked Quail, who was tying a hatbox on to the very top of the pile.

'Yes, sire,' Quail replied wearily. 'And your slippers with the bells on them and your extra-cosy blanket.'

King Cudgel chewed his lip. 'What about—?'

'Your supply of sugar lumps, sire?' asked Quail.

King Cudgel nodded and stared at his feet.

'Four bowls filled to the brim and an emergency sack,' said Quail. He looked pityingly at the king. 'Just in case you get lost in the forest and have to leave a trail behind you.'

'Well done, Quail!' cried the king, feeling better for the first time that day. 'What would I do without you?'

Quail couldn't imagine. He shrugged his shoulders and went back to his packing.

At the far end of the castle garden in his snack shack, Prince Marvin was putting the finishing touches to his pile of supplies. Beside him, Princess Gusty Ox was ticking off a list.

'Flour? Rice? Spaghetti?'

'Check.'

'Spices? Sugar? Herbs?'

'Check.'

'Your yummy homemade sausages?'
Princess Gusty Ox smiled at her brother
and he smiled back.

'Double check.'

'Puddings and sweeties?'

'Check.'

'Fresh vegetables?'

'Absolutely not.'

Princess Gusty Ox put down her pen. 'That's it. We're ready.' She heaved a long stick, hanging with cooking pots, frying pans and ladles, over her shoulder, checked her pocket axe was securely fixed to her belt and went out into the garden.

Prince Marvin was just about to follow when a strange idea suddenly popped into his head. He took down a small, lumpy sack from the shelf and stuffed it in his pocket. Then he firmly shut the door and followed his sister to the castle yard.

No one in the royal party knew what to expect as they went deeper and deeper into the forest, but as the king's cart trundled over the narrow path, the trees seemed to close behind them as if they were walking into a prison.

Almost immediately, King Cudgel decided to hide under his blanket. He didn't like forests at the best of times and had never actually been into the one behind Crunchbone Castle. It was more frightening than he had ever imagined. He closed his eyes and pretended he was on his way to spend a day at the seaside.

As Princess Gusty Ox and Prince Marvin walked through the trees, they noticed with sinking hearts that all the birds seemed to be flying away as fast as they could. When they looked at their feet, the ground seemed to be alive with mice and hedgehogs and squirrels, also trying to escape.

'It's almost as if they know something terrible might happen,' muttered Prince Marvin to his sister.

The only terrible thing Princess Gusty Ox could imagine was that when the moment came for her to stab the Bear Witch with the silver arrow, for some reason she would miss. But it was such a dreadful thought, she couldn't bring herself to tell her brother. So she nodded and said nothing.

∞

Three hours later, the donkey pulling King Cudgel and his cart stopped in a small clearing.

'Are you sure it's safe here?' asked the king. He poked his head out from under his blanket and peered around.

'Nothing's safe in the forest, sire,' said Quail. 'You wait in the cart until I've set up your private tent.'

'Good man, Quail,' said the king, reaching in his pocket for a handful of sugar lumps. Then he hid under his blanket again.

On the other side of the clearing, Princess Gusty Ox lowered the pole with the pots and pans to the ground. As she had been walking through the forest, she had also been thinking about what Crackle had told them of the Bear Witch's spell. Even if she didn't miss with the silver arrow, there was still one big problem.

'How are we are going to tell the difference between our mother and the Bear Witch?' Princess Gusty Ox asked Prince Marvin, as he handed her a stick of dried deer meat to chew.

'I wouldn't worry about that,' Prince Marvin smiled at his sister. 'Remember what Crackle told us. We'll know what to do when the time comes.'

Prince Marvin held out another stick of dried meat. He knew Princess Gusty Ox was always extra hungry when she was extra worried. 'Besides, they might not look *absolutely* the same. There might be a tiny difference that only *we* will be able to spot.'

'I hope you're right,' replied Princess Gusty Ox.

Prince Marvin looked straight into his sister's unhappy face. 'So do I,' he said quietly.

Chapter Four

An hour later, Princess Gusty Ox was more downhearted than ever. After her talk with Prince Marvin, she had gone into the forest. The princess was one of the best trackers in the kingdom and she hadn't found a single strange print *anywhere*.

Now, as she helped Quail put up her father's private tent, Princess Gusty Ox began to worry that they wouldn't be able to find the Bear Witch *or* her mother. And if they couldn't find them, they wouldn't have a chance to work out who was who and Queen Carrion would be doomed to be half human, half bear for ever.

Princess Gusty Ox thought back over her years of hunting, shooting, spearing and fishing. She thought of all the different ways she had tracked down animals and suddenly she remembered an old hunter's saying: *if you can't trap 'em, trick 'em.*

'Bait!' she said out loud. 'That'll bring them to us!'

'Bring who?' snarled Quail, looking murderously at the king, who was smoothing down the sides of the snowy

white doublet he had just changed into for a campfire supper. 'Bait what?'

'Sorry, Quail,' replied Princess Gusty Ox as she whacked the final tent peg into the ground with her fist. 'I was thinking aloud.

You see, I didn't find any strange bear tracks in the forest, and if we're going to save the queen in time, we'll have to lure her and the Bear Witch to our campsite.'

'How?' asked Quail suspiciously.

'We'll use bait,' repeated Princess Gusty Ox. 'You know. Rotten meat. Irresistible smells. That sort of thing.'

At that moment, Prince Marvin walked up to them with a huge grin on his face. 'I heard every word you said, sis,' he said. 'And you're absolutely right.' He patted Princess Gusty Ox's thick, strong arms. 'Leave it to me. I know exactly what to do.'

∞

The next morning, while King Cudgel was still asleep in his private tent, Prince Marvin called Princess Gusty Ox from the campfire.

'Hey, sis! Come and look at these!'

Princess Gusty Ox jumped out of her wolf-skin hammock and ran over the stony ground. The next minute she was staring at two sets of prints and a shiver went right through her. There were the outlines of toes and the shapes of claws!

The prints were obviously half bear and half human!

'They were here in the night,' whispered Princess Gusty Ox. 'Did you put out any bait?'

Prince Marvin shook his head. 'They must have just been curious.' He grinned at his sister. 'But we'll get them this evening for sure!'

King Cudgel woke up, trembling from head to toe. 'But I *can't*,' he shouted out loud. 'I just *can't!*' He reached wildly for a handful of sugar lumps, but to his horror his emergency bedside casket was empty.

'What can't you do, sire?' asked Quail as he dragged the sack of sugar lumps into the royal tent and filled up the empty casket.

'I can't be the one who holds the arrow,' cried King Cudgel, grabbing the bowl and tipping the whole lot into his mouth.

The sound of crunching was deafening so Quail waited until it was over.

'Of course, you can't,' he said in a soothing voice. 'Everyone knows that aiming straight isn't your thing. Princess Gusty Ox will look after that. Besides, she's the only one who's strong enough.'

'But I still have to *try* to help save the queen!' The king's wrinkled, parsnip nose quivered horribly. 'I knew that the moment I realised she was the bear in my dream.'

'Anything you say, sire,' muttered Quail. 'Anything you say. I'll find you a normal arrow and you can practise throwing.' He picked up the magic silver one and wrapped it up in a piece of red velvet. 'Just don't touch the real thing in case you bend it.'

All day, King Cudgel practised throwing the arrow, even though he only once hit the enormous target Quail had built for him. And that was because he cheated.

Still, Prince Marvin and Princess Gusty Ox did their best to encourage their father. They both knew he wanted to help as much everyone else. More importantly, they knew the magic silver arrow was safe.

But by sunset, everyone was getting very, very worried. Despite all the different things Prince Marvin had cooked up on the fire and despite all the traps Princess Gusty Ox had laid, there was still no sign of Queen Carrion and the Bear Witch.

Everyone could see the moon was almost full and that meant time was running out.

'What are we going to do if they don't show up?' Princess Gusty Ox said to her brother, as she sat by the fire chewing her fingernails.

'Mother will never resist *this*,' said Prince Marvin firmly. He pointed to a huge pot of bubbling stew. 'It's goat's knuckle stew flavoured with tree fungus. She ate it for lunch the day she disappeared.'

As he spoke, he lifted the lid on the great pot and wafted the rich, goaty smell into the forest with an old blanket. Then, just in case, he picked up the small, lumpy sack he had taken down from the shelf, emptied it into a small pot and poured boiling water over the top.

At that moment, Princess Gusty Ox saw something flicker in the dusky light and grabbed a spear. At first, it looked like fireflies behind an extra-big tree, and then she realised the twinkling lights were in pairs.

Two pairs!

Princess Gusty Ox nearly dropped the spear on her foot. 'Marv,' she whispered, jerking her head towards the tree. 'Don't look now, but I think we've got company!'

Chapter Five

'Cudgel!' cried two gruff voices. Two barrel-sized, bear-like Queen Carrions with fierce, brown eyes, furry arms and legs, and both wearing tunics, cloaks and a crown walked into the clearing at exactly the same time. 'What took you so long?'

King Cudgel, Prince Marvin, Princess Gusty Ox and Quail all stared. It was worse than anything they had expected. Not only did the two creatures in front of them *look* identical, they appeared to do and say everything at the same time, too. Yet one of them was Queen Carrion!

How would they ever tell them apart?

'Mother?' croaked Princess Gusty Ox, looking hopelessly from one to the other.

'Gusty Pops,' said the two bear-like Queen Carrions in hoarse, cooing voices. 'Come and give mummy a hug.' They smiled yellow-toothed smiles at the same time and held out their hairy arms. 'She won't bite you!'

Princess Gusty Ox turned to Prince Marvin. 'They know my nickname,' she said in a horrified voice.

'Of course they do,' muttered Prince Marvin. 'One of them's our mother, but she's never cooed in her life.'

'Stop whispering!' roared the two bear-like Queen Carrions. 'It's rude!' They whirled around to King Cudgel, who was standing wringing his hands. 'Well? Haven't you got anything to say?'

'You haven't given me a chance,' cried King Cudgel in a hurt voice.

'Yes, we did,' shouted the two bear-like Queen Carrions.

'No, you didn't,' cried the king.

Princess Gusty Ox looked at Prince Marvin. Things were not going well at all.

'One of them is playing for time,' whispered Princess Gusty Ox.

'But who?' replied Prince Marvin. His eyes looked sideways at the cooking pot. Surely only his mother would want to eat goat's knuckle stew. It was absolutely disgusting. 'Dinner time!' he cried.

'Mmm! Goat's knuckle stew,' cried both bear-like Queen Carrions. They sat down at a picnic table and began greedily slurping up spoonfuls at exactly the same time. 'Yum! Taste that tree fungus!'

'Marvin made it specially for you, mother,' said Princess Gusty Ox looking at the two sets of brown eyes and desperately hoping she would recognise her mother in one of them.

'Clever Marvy,' growled the two bear-like Queen Carrions. 'It was our last lunch.'

At the end of the table, King Cudgel had turned to sugar lumps to calm himself down. He knew it was his turn to try to tell them apart. 'Do you remember our first dance, dearest?' he said to the space between the two bear queens.

'How could we forget,' they replied. 'You promised us your kingdom if we'd get off your foot.'

King Cudgel gave up and shot Quail a pleading look.

Quail stood up and made a show of clattering the dishes in a pile. Like everyone else, he wanted to help save Queen Carrion. So, just before dinner, he had unwrapped up the silver arrow and put it in his pocket. Now, as he went around the table handing out bowls and spoons for pudding, Princess Gusty Ox felt something thin and sharp being slipped into her belt.

She knew immediately it was the arrow but she still had no idea which of the two bear queens was her mother and which was the Bear Witch!

Princess Gusty Ox looked hopelessly at her brother.

Prince Marvin picked up a small, yellow cooking pot with a lid and put it on the table. 'Surprise pudding!' he cried. '*Everyone's* favourite!'

As Prince Marvin handed the ladle to Quail, he whispered quickly in his ear. Then he caught his sister's eye and behind the two bear-like Queen Carrions, he made the sign of a T with his fingers.

Princess Gusty Ox heart's banged in her chest! The sign of the T meant only one thing. *Tapioca*!

Everyone in Crunchbone Castle hated it. But Queen Carrion hated it more than anything else in the whole world.

She hated its taste.

She hated its colour.

But most of all she hated the way it felt like frog spawn as soon as you put it in your mouth.

Princess Gusty Ox secretly pulled out the arrow from her belt and held it in her hand like a dart. Then she sat absolutely still and fixed her eyes on both bear-like

Queen Carrions. Up until now, the two of them had behaved in exactly the same way at the same time. Now Princess Gusty Ox was hoping against hope that one would show a sign of disgust first.

And that one would be her mother.

In slow motion, Quail opened the lid of the pot. 'TAPIOCA!' he bellowed.

The bear-like Queen Carrion on the left snorted with disgust. A split-second later the one the right did the same!

But it was too late! Princess Gusty Ox pulled back her meaty arm and threw. Her aim was perfect! The arrow sank deep into the black, furry heart of the Bear Witch.

To everyone's utter astonishment, instead of a roar, there was a huge POP! And what had been the Bear Witch rose into the sky with a noise like a punctured balloon.

At that moment, a full moon spread a dazzling silver light over the clearing. At first it was so bright no one could see anything, but then Quail noticed the outline of a giant frog in a pointy hat sailing down through the stars!

It was Crackle!

The wizard landed on the ground and held out his hands. Bolts of purple and blue light shot from his fingers and the bear-like Queen Carrion turned back into a real queen!

Suddenly the whole forest was full of the sounds of birds chirping and squirrels chattering in the branches. All the animals had come back. The Bear Witch's spell was well and truly broken!

Queen Carrion jumped up and wrapped her arms around King Cudgel's neck. 'Thank you for rescuing me,' she cried. 'I've been hoping and hoping you would come.'

The queen turned to Princess Gusty Ox and Prince Marvin and held out her arms. Neither the prince nor princess could believe their eyes. Their mother had never, ever done that before. For a moment they hesitated. Then they ran to her and felt her huge, powerful arms wrap themselves around them and hold them tight.

It was like being hugged by a bear!

Queen Carrion laughed as she guessed what was in their minds. 'Gusty Pops! Marvy!' she murmured in their ears. 'I've missed you so much.'

Then she sat back and looked at them all in turn. 'I've had a lot of time to do a lot of thinking,' she said in a serious voice. 'That Bear Witch had a terrible temper, you know. She used to shout and swear at me so much that sometimes the air turned purple around her. And do you know what?'

'What?' asked Prince Marvin nervously.

'She reminded me of myself,' said Queen Carrion. 'And I suddenly realised what a bad-tempered old bag I've been for years.'

'Your Majesty,' protested Quail. 'Surely not.'

'Yes, Quail,' said Queen Carrion, firmly. 'I have been almost impossible to live with and you know it's true.'

'But sweetest,' cried King Cudgel, after Quail had prodded him. 'We're just happy to have you back. We don't care if you're a—'

Suddenly, his mouth filled with sugar lumps and everyone, including Crackle, who hadn't made magic so fast for years, heaved a sigh of relief.

Queen Carrion laughed. And Princess Gusty Ox and Prince Marvin realised with astonishment that it was the first time they had ever heard such a thing.

'Well, *I* care, Cudgel, dear,' she said. 'Because from now on, everything's going to be different.' She paused and a big smile spread across her face. 'I'm giving up my sword and I'm never going bear hunting again. After all, that was what got me into trouble in the first place!'

As she spoke, Queen Carrion opened her arms again and looked around at her family. This time, there was no hesitation.

Princess Gusty Ox and Prince Marvin threw their arms around her and King Cudgel planted a big sugary kiss on her cheek!

They were one big happy family again. Just as the picture in the smoke from Crackle's pointy hat had foretold!